Hurricane Summer

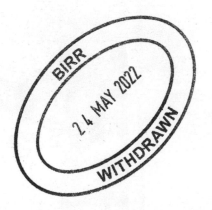

Read all the books in Robert Swindells'

World War II Trilogy

Doodlebug Alley
Hurricane Summer
Roger's War

Hurricane Summer

Robert Swindells

AWARD PUBLICATIONS LIMITED

ISBN 978-1-78270-161-3

Illustrated by Kim Palmer
Cover illustration by Leo Hartas

This edition published by Award Publications Limited 2015

Published by Award Publications Limited,
The Old Riding School, The Welbeck Estate,
Worksop, Nottinghamshire, S80 3LR

www.awardpublications.co.uk

15 1

Printed in the United Kingdom

For Chloe

K.P.

Contents

One

Funny things, friendships. They tend to come and go, but most people have a special friend who stands out among all the others. I'm lucky – I've got two. One of them's been dead a long time now, but it doesn't matter – he'll always be my friend. As for the other … well, as I said, friendships are funny. Best thing I can do is tell you about them.

World War II was on and I was ten. I was an only child. My dad had been killed the previous autumn serving with the Navy. Mum said I must always remember that my dad had been a hero, and I knew he

9

had, and that was the trouble.

You see, I wasn't a hero. Far from it.

There was this lad at school. Clive Simcox. He was the same age as me – we were in the same class – but Clive was taller and heavier and for some reason that summer he started picking on me. I didn't like fighting so I was forever trying to please him. I let him win at marbles and lent him my wicket keeper's gloves. I even gave him my best stamp – a Guadeloupe triangular – but it was no use. He'd still ambush me on the way home from school and bash me up. He used to wait for me in the mornings too, and trip me as I ran past. I'd arrive at school with grazed knees and dirt on my blazer and red eyes from crying, and everybody would know Clive had had another go at me.

Up until then, the war had been terrific fun for me. I know it's an awful thing to say, but you've got to remember that village life in the thirties was pretty boring, especially if you were a kid. Think about it. People didn't travel much in those days. Not like now. There were people in the village – old people – who'd never seen the sea. It's true. So a kid born in the village could expect to spend all his life there.

Imagine that. You're nine years old and you already know every inch of the place. You know everybody who lives there too, and they know you. Everything goes on pretty much the way it always has, so it stands to reason nothing exciting is ever going to happen to you. Nothing unexpected. Most kids even knew what job they'd do for the rest of their lives once they left school. And of course there was no TV or video games or anything like that. Kids today don't know what boring is.

So, when the war came along and things started happening, we lapped it up. Oh, the adults put on grave expressions and went round tutting and shaking their heads, but most of them were loving it too, deep down. You could tell. It broke up the routine, and people tend to welcome that, even if they pretend otherwise.

There was no actual danger. Not at first. The beginning of the war was very quiet – so quiet that people called it the phoney war. You see, we'd expected waves of bombers. Poison gas. Invasion. Our shelters were ready and everybody had a gas mask. We'd stuck sticky tape across our windows so glass wouldn't fly. There were even some kids in the village who'd been evacuated from London.

It was these preparations for war we found exciting. Council workmen came and dug an enormous hole near the High Street to

make a public shelter. Some of our teachers joined the Local Defence Volunteers and were to be seen in the evenings, drilling on the Green with dummy rifles. That was fun to watch – somebody yelling at them for a change. And school itself was exciting because our lessons were interrupted by gas-mask practice and shelter drill.

But the best thing was the aerodrome, which was outside the village. It was a tiny one belonging to a flying club, but in 1938 the Air Ministry had taken it over and now it was being transformed. Its bumpy grass runway had been ploughed up and replaced by two proper ones. A second hangar was in the process of being built, together with

15

rows and rows of long wooden huts on land requisitioned from adjoining farms. Ginger Kitteridge and I used to bike over there and watch. My dad was still alive then and Clive Simcox hadn't started bullying me, so I was pretty carefree. It's a good job none of us knows the future, isn't it?

We played games of course, same as before, except now our favourite game was soldiers. We'd pick sides and toss a coin. If you lost the toss you had to be the Germans, which meant you couldn't win.

The village was our battleground. The British would chase the Germans along the High Street and in and out of gardens, yards and alleyways. The Germans cheated a lot – hiding inside the church or ganging up five against one – but the British always fought fair. Our battles usually

ended on the Green, where the Germans would be caught in the open and mown down with tommy guns. They always died dramatically – throwing up their arms and rolling over three or four times in the grass before finally coming to rest. There were benches here and there round the rim of the Green and sometimes, on warm days, the climax of the battle would be watched by a few old villagers sitting out enjoying the sunshine.

On the particular day I want to tell you about, Sam Drury was there, twitching and blinking as usual.

Sam was the village barber, and we weren't supposed to stare at him. It was hard not to, because of the twitching and blinking. Sam had fought in the trenches in World War I and had shellshock. Us kids weren't sure what that meant, but our parents said he'd come home from Flanders twenty years ago twitching and blinking and hadn't stopped since. It didn't keep him from being a good barber, but it was hard not to crack up laughing when he was cutting your hair and you could see him in the mirror.

Anyway, this particular day he was on one of the benches, and I was a German. When I got shot, I fell with a cry and rolled over and over, coming to rest spread-eagled on my back with my eyes shut. I was lying there, listening to the British making tommy gun noises, when a voice whispered, 'You never get up, you know, once you're down.'

I opened my eyes and saw Sam Drury looking down at me. I hadn't realised I was so close to his bench.

'P-pardon?'

He blinked rapidly. 'I said, you never get up once you're down. Not when it's real.'

'I … I know that, Mr Drury.' I could feel my cheeks going red. 'We're playing, that's all. It's just a game.'

'A game. Yes.' He gazed across the Green. The Germans were all dead. The British were standing at a distance, staring at Sam.

'We thought it was a game in 1914,' he murmured. 'Couldn't wait to enlist.' He smiled crookedly. 'It was the girls, you see. And the songs. "Goodbye, Dolly Grey". "Tipperary". They made us feel like heroes. Should've seen us, lad, marching through the village. Bags of swank.' He shook his head. 'Different down Salisbury Plain though, and when we finally reached the Front we thought we'd arrived in Hell. Wounded on stretchers in the mud, blind and screaming. Dead mules, bloated and covered in flies. The filthy, inescapable stink. Gulping rum at dawn so you'd be drunk enough to go over the top instead of lying in the bottom of the trench blubbing for your ma, which is what you'd do if you was sober. Don't show none of that, do

they, in their recruiting posters? Ain't no songs about it neither.'

He sniffled, wiping his cheek with the back of his hand. 'It's goodbye Dolly Grey though – they got that bit right.' He slumped forward, dangling his hands between his knees. 'She don't want you no more, see? Not when you can't hold your head still nor stop blinking.'

He was crying. There's nothing more embarrassing to a kid than a grown-up crying. I didn't know where to put myself. What to say. The other Germans had stopped being dead and were standing with the British, staring across at us. I got up quietly. Sam Drury seemed to have forgotten I was there and I tiptoed away. But whenever I played soldiers after that, I kept thinking about the stuff he'd mentioned.

Spoiled it a bit, I can tell you, but not as much as something that happened a few weeks later.

Two

I don't know if I told you, but my dad was in the Navy. He'd been in the Volunteer Reserve, and he joined up the day after war broke out. We got letters from him at Chatham, then Greenwich, then Scotland where he was serving on HMS *Royal Oak*. One day – it was October 15th 1939 – Mum got a telegram. Dad was dead.

She couldn't believe it at first, and neither could I. It didn't seem real. He'd only been gone a month, and his ship had been at the British Naval Base at Scapa Flow. It turned out an enemy submarine had sneaked in and torpedoed her as she lay at anchor. Hundreds of sailors died, and my dad was one of them. He was our village's first casualty.

I'd be lying if I said his death ruined my life. I loved him – don't think I didn't – and I suppose I missed him for a time, but kids are resilient. They get over things amazingly quickly. I cried a bit at first, but within a couple of weeks I was biking to and from school and messing about with my chums as if nothing had happened.

Mind you, it must've been absolutely rotten for Mum. People rallied round of course, but still, she must have been deeply unhappy and horribly lonely, and I can't have helped. I expected my togs washed and ironed, breakfast on the table, same as before. And I got it, and took it all for

granted. She might have cried all night,
but there she'd be in the morning to see me
fed, straighten my hair and tuck a clean

27

handkerchief in my pocket. She even found a smile for me most mornings. When we hear the term war hero we think of soldiers, sailors and airmen, but my mother was a war hero, and she got no decoration, unless you count the Wooden Cross, and she had to wait for that till she was dead.

Mind you, there were funny things as well as sad ones. There was this lad in our class – Roger Fallowfield. He was none too bright and the kids were always having him on. He was a great, clumsy lad but he was mad about the Army. 'Oh, I hope the war goes on,' he'd groan about ten times a day. 'I hope it doesn't stop before I'm old enough to join the Army.'

One day he said this to Frank Littlejohn. Now Frank was a bit of a practical joker and he looked at Roger and said, 'You

don't have to be eighteen, you know. Not now. They've formed this new regiment. The Infantry, they call it, 'cause infants can join.'

Well, old Roger gaped at him and said, 'Is that right, Frankie? You're not having me on, are you?'

'Would I joke about the British Army, old son?' says Frank. 'There's been a lot of casualties, see? They're running out of eighteen-year-olds so they've decided to start taking kids. You toddle off down to the Recruiting Office and I bet they'll welcome you with open arms.'

There was a Recruiting Office in Bromley, our nearest town. Saturday morning, Roger was standing outside when it opened. He'd brushed his shoes and combed his hair, and in he went. There was a big sergeant sitting behind a desk.

'Now then, sonny,' says the sergeant, 'what can we do for you?'

'Please, sir,' says Roger, 'I've come to join the Army.'

The sergeant sighs and shakes his head. 'Go away, son,' he says, 'I'm a busy man.'

'But I mean it,' says poor Roger. 'I've come to volunteer.'

The sergeant sighs and starts to get up. Anybody can see he's getting mad – anybody but Roger, that is. 'How old are you?' growls the sergeant.

'Eleven,' says Roger, 'but that's all right, 'cause I want that new regiment that takes kids – you know – the Infantry.'

Well, the sergeant came round that desk like greased lightning and chased poor old Roger halfway down the High Street. Frank Littlejohn had shadowed Roger to see what would happen and he told us all about it on Monday. Said the sergeant looked like a mad gorilla. We laughed for days.

Then there was Sludgy Meedles. Sludgy was a pig farmer, and he was cheating the government. See – meat was rationed, and farmers were supposed to tell the government how many piglets they were

rearing, or lambs, or calves, but Sludgy cheated. What he'd do was, he'd say nine piglets had been born when there were really ten. He did this all the time, so there were loads of unofficial pigs in a secret sty in a far corner of the farm. Everybody knew he was doing it but nobody could prove it. Every now and then a van would visit Sludgy's place in the middle of the night

and carry off a pig or two. The old rogue got pots of dosh for those pigs, I can tell you.

Anyway, one sunny afternoon a pilot got into difficulties just after he'd taken off and had to crash-land on Sludgy's farm.

The Hurricane went slithering across a bumpy field and smashed right into the secret pigsty. The pilot was OK but the

plane was a write-off and the countryside was swarming with terrified, squealing piglets. The police came to round them up and, as these were unofficial pigs, Sludgy couldn't admit they were his. 'Not mine, Constable,' he says. 'Never seen 'em before

in my life.' So the police carted 'em off and that was that. Whole village had a laugh about it, 'cept Sludgy.

Three

Anyway I started off telling you about Clive Simcox so I'll get back to him. He bashed me up as I said, but he used to make remarks about my dad, which was even worse. Before the war Dad had been an electrician, so they made him an electrician in the Navy. I don't know what his work was exactly, but it had to do with electrical circuits and that sort of thing. Anyway, Simcox had latched on to this and sometimes he'd say, 'He was nothing special, you know, your dad. He wasn't a gunner or a torpedo man. He didn't kill any Germans. He was just an electrician, mending fuses and changing lightbulbs while other fellows did the fighting.' This would be in the playground or on the street and he'd say it at the top of his voice so everyone could hear, and all the time he'd be pushing me – shoving me in the chest so that I had to keep stepping backwards. He was goading me of course – trying to make me fight, but I was too scared. Red-faced with shame, I'd retreat till he got bored and went off to bother somebody else.

I despised myself. I'd think, what sort of kid doesn't stick up for his dead father? Defend his honour? If I was half the hero Dad was, I'd stand up to Simcox and punch him on the nose, even if he bashed me up after. Sometimes, lying in bed in the morning I'd convince myself that this time I was going to do it. This time I'd turn with my fists up and give him the biggest surprise of his life, but I never did. When it came to it – when he was actually there in

front of me with his red face and mocking eyes – I'd either try to run or let him hit me to get it over with. I was ashamed of myself but I couldn't help it.

Funniest thing was, Simcox senior wasn't even in the forces. He worked in a button factory, but I daren't bring that up when Clive was tormenting me. Shows how scared I was, and believe me it's no joke being a coward when the world seems full of heroes.

Our world was full of heroes all right. The aerodrome was three times its pre-war size and three squadrons of Hurricanes were stationed there. Picton Hill, it was called. RAF Picton Hill. It's part of the industrial estate now, but in 1940 it was famous.

Pilots from Picton Hill were often to be seen driving or cycling along the High

Street or sitting on the Green outside The Bull, laughing and yarning. In 1940 fighter pilots were the public's idols – the equivalent of pop stars or soccer heroes today. They knew it too, some of them. They'd roar through the village in flashy, open-top sports cars, wearing brightly coloured silk scarves and with the top button of their tunics left undone to show who they were. To us boys they were gods. We'd gawp at them from a distance, longing for a nod or a wink or a word. In 1940, every schoolboy in England wanted to be a fighter pilot.

One hot afternoon, when I got in from school, I found Mum talking with one of these idols in the garden. I'd managed to dodge Clive for once, so I was fairly presentable. 'Jim,' smiled Mum, 'this is Pilot Officer Cochrane. He helped me home with my shopping.'

I was completely bowled over. Pilot Officer Cochrane really looked like a hero. Tall he was, and slim, with black hair and a tanned face. I'd never been close to a fighter pilot before, and when he stuck out his hand I stood gaping.

'Well, Jim?' laughed Mum. 'Aren't you

going to shake hands?'

'Uh? Oh yes – sorry.' I shoved my paw out and he gripped it, grinning. His teeth were dazzlingly white. I wondered fleetingly what he'd think if he knew he was shaking hands with a coward.

'Name's Mike,' he said, 'but my friends call me Cocky. I hope we're going to be friends, Jim.'

I could hardly believe it. A fighter pilot for a friend. They'd be green with envy at school. I looked at him. 'Do you spy a Flitfire – I mean, fly a Spitfire?'

He roared with laughter. Mum laughed too. I felt myself blushing.

'No,' he chuckled. 'I don't spy a Flitfire – I high a Flurricane.'

He stayed for tea. It was only sardines on toast, but I wished it could last for ever.

He was really nice, and not a bit conceited. I was sure if I had wings on my tunic I'd be very conceited indeed.

Four

I couldn't wait to tell my chums next morning. By a wizard stroke of luck, Simcox missed me again so I was able to shove all that beastliness to the back of my mind while I basked in Cocky's reflected glory.

'He didn't,' gasped Ginger Kitteridge, when I told them Cocky had stayed for tea.

I smirked. 'He did, so there. And he said he hoped we'd be friends.'

You should have seen their faces.

I told them about one of Cocky's exploits. He hadn't mentioned any exploits at all so I had to make one up, but I knew it was

exactly the sort of thing he'd do.

'Once,' I told the spellbound circle, which included Simcox, 'flying alone on a dawn patrol, Cocky spotted a formation of 110s. There were nine of them, but he didn't hesitate. Putting his Hurricane into a shallow dive, he got their leader in his sights and blasted him out of the sky with a burst from his eight Brownings.'

The kids gasped and I glowed, bragging about my friend. 'As the leader disintegrated,' I said, 'Cocky flew right through the formation and came up underneath them, firing at another 110. This one flipped on its back, trailing smoke, and the pilot baled out. Levelling off, Cocky shot a third Nazi out of the sky then zoomed into the clouds, escaping before the remaining six knew what was happening.'

'Wow!' they went, and 'Golly!' I was flavour of the month, though we didn't have that expression in those days. It cut no ice with Simcox though. He went on tormenting me and I went on letting him, imagining Cocky's reproachful eyes watching me now as well as Dad's.

Cocky started spending most of his free

time at our house. I realise now that he must have been sweet on Mum, but I didn't at the time. I thought he came to see me. And we did become friends. He made me a kite, which we flew together, and we went fishing too. Mum came with us sometimes, and sometimes it was just him and me. I loved being with him. I was proud to be seen in

his company, as any boy would have been.
The only slightly disappointing thing was
that I could never get him to talk about his

flying. I'd ask him things and he'd change the subject. He didn't get stroppy about it – I don't mean that – but he obviously preferred not to talk about it. But that was about to change.

Five

One day we were flying the kite. It was a perfect day for it – breezy, with scudding clouds and sudden bursts of sunshine – but I couldn't stop thinking about Simcox and it was spoiling my day. Mum wasn't with us, so when we knocked off for the sandwiches and a flask of tea I decided to make a clean breast of it. 'Cocky,' I said, 'I wish I was fearless like you.'

He was winding the kite-string round the bit of dowelling we used for a handgrip. He laughed, glancing down at me. It was a short laugh, and there was no humour in it.

'Fearless?' He finished winding and handed me the kite. 'I'm not fearless, Jim. I'm petrified. Permanently petrified.'

I shook my head. I assumed he was joking. He was one of those people who can joke with a perfectly straight face.

'Oh yeah?' I grinned. 'Whoever heard of a petrified fighter pilot?'

'Nobody's heard, Jim,' he said. 'Everybody thinks we're fearless because that's what the newspapers say, but it's not true.' He sat down beside me, looking away towards the aerodrome. I put the kite down and started unwrapping the sandwiches.

After a minute he said, 'The papers have to say we're fearless to keep people's spirits up, but we're not. None of us.' He plucked a stalk of grass and chewed the end. He wasn't looking at me.

'Do you know what happens when a
Hurricane catches fire, Jim?'

I shook my head. I'd seen planes come
down in flames – we all had, but they were
always a long way off.

Cocky went on gazing towards the
aerodrome. 'What happens,' he said quietly,

'is that the fuel burns. Gallons and gallons of high-octane fuel. The slipstream blows the flames into the cockpit like a blowtorch, right into the pilot's face. If he gets out at once he might escape with blistered hands and cheeks. If he doesn't – and it usually takes a while to undo the harness and get the

canopy off – those flames'll have destroyed his face and maybe his eyes as well. If he gets out then – if the pain hasn't caused him to faint and if the plane's not spinning, pinning him in the cockpit by centrifugal force – he's going to walk around for the rest of his life looking like something out of a horror story, even if he's not blind. He's going to catch people staring at him, then looking away quickly when they see he's noticed. He'll see people turn sick at the mere sight of him, and, of course, he's never going to kiss a pretty girl again.'

He shook his head. 'Mind you, they don't always burn. A man might die in the cockpit, riddled with bullets or blown in two by a cannon shell, or sit screaming as his crippled plane spins into the sea.'

He flung the stem away. 'One of those things happens to somebody every time we scramble, Jim, and we sometimes scramble four, five, six times a day. And while we're sitting around waiting for the call, we're thinking about the things I've just mentioned – about chums who've bought it recently. Remembering how old George, who used to be so handsome, looked in hospital with his lips and nose and eyelids gone, knowing that sooner or later it'll be our turn.'

Cocky lay down with his hands behind his head and gazed into the sky. 'And that's not the worst of it, Jim. The nights are the worst, because no matter how tired you are – and I've never known such tiredness – it's almost impossible to sleep. Your thoughts won't let you sleep. Is it my turn tomorrow? Will I burn? Will this bed be empty twenty-four hours from now? And if you do drop off from sheer exhaustion, there are the nightmares.'

He turned his head to look at me. 'And you think I'm fearless, Jim? You think I'm not afraid?' He snorted. 'I've puked laddie – got up out of my bed and thrown up at the mere thought of ever flying again. I'll tell you this, Jim. If I could – if I dared – I'd get up right now and start running,

and I wouldn't stop till I was somewhere they'd never find me. And that's true of all fighter pilots – every one of us.' He sat up, wrapped his arms round his bony shins and rested his forehead on his knees. 'Only the insane are fearless, Jim. The rest of us carry on because we're trapped.'

I never did tell him about Simcox. I suppose his story made my problem seem piddling. It made me feel better though, knowing Cocky was afraid. Knowing I wasn't the only one. It certainly put paid to my illusions about the glamour of war in the air, and it did something else as well. It caused me to watch Cocky closely whenever he was with us, and it quickly became evident that he'd told me the truth.

To those who didn't know, including Mum, he remained the dashing, dare-devil character with the infectious grin – a big, gangly schoolboy for whom the war, or at least his bit of it, was nothing but a ripping adventure. But if you were watching, the

signs were there. The way he perched on the very edge of his chair. That twitchy eyelid. The lower lip caught between his teeth and the expression of utter desolation when he thought nobody was looking.

And don't think it made me any less fond of him, because it didn't. Quite the opposite in fact. He'd confided in me. Told me things he wouldn't tell anybody else in the world. We were best friends.

Six

One afternoon, just before the start of the summer holidays, I was helping Mum get the tea when there was a knock on the open door. We looked round and saw a pilot on the step. He didn't say anything. He just stood holding his cap in both hands, looking at Mum. Mum gazed back for a moment, then said in a quiet voice, 'It's Cocky, isn't it?'

The pilot nodded, stepping into the sunny kitchen. 'This morning,' he murmured, 'near Deal. I am most awfully sorry.' And Mum began to cry. I stared from one to the

other till it sank in, then ran howling to my room.

I don't know if you've ever lost your best friend. I hope not. If you haven't, it's no use me trying to describe to you how I felt. You'd have to feel it for yourself. Anyway I was ill all night and Mum kept me off school the next day, and in the middle of the morning there was an air raid.

I was in bed thinking about Cocky when the siren went. Mum was down the village but that was OK – they weren't after the village. It was the aerodrome they wanted. It wasn't the first raid we'd had, and everybody knew what to do. There was a shelter at the bottom of our garden – an Anderson shelter, which Mum and I shared with the people next door. Whenever the siren went we'd drop what we were doing,

hurry down the garden and sit in the damp
shelter, waiting for the all-clear. We'd hear
the planes go over, and those dull, flat
bangs bombs make, mingled with the noise
of the ack-ack guns. The Nazis hoped to
catch the RAF unawares and destroy our

fighters on the ground, but the Hurricanes nearly always scrambled before they arrived, and there'd be dog-fights. I always wanted to watch, but Mum would never let

me leave the shelter so I'd have to make do with listening to the machine guns, which sounding like cloth tearing.

After the all-clear, kids would rush out looking for bomb-tails and bits of shrapnel to add to their collections. At the aerodrome there'd be a few fresh holes in the runway and perhaps a building on fire.

Anyway there I was in bed, and the siren went and I decided not to go to the shelter. I didn't particularly want to die, but I wasn't bothered one way or the other and Mum wasn't there to make me go. I got up and went into Mum's room, which faced the aerodrome. I waited till Mrs Mullins next door was in the shelter, then perched on the sill to watch.

I didn't actually see much. The church and its stand of ancient yews formed a

sort of screen between our house and the
aerodrome. I heard the engines and the
detonations as usual, but all I saw was one
plane – I think it was a Junkers 88 – and
a coil of oily smoke beyond the spire. The
whole thing lasted about five minutes, then
it went quiet, and after a bit the all-clear

sounded and I could hear the Hurricanes coming in to land.

I went back to bed. Half an hour later Mum came in. She'd been in the public shelter under the High Street.

'They hit a house,' she said, 'in Oasthouse Lane.' She said it in a flat, uninterested voice, and I knew she was grieving for Cocky.

Next day – it was Friday, the last day before the hols – I was trailing along the lane when suddenly Clive Simcox sprang out in front of me and snatched my cap. I don't know to this day what came over me, but before I knew what I was doing I'd clenched my fist and smashed it into the middle of Clive's face. He must've been really startled because he neither struck back nor covered up, but stood there gaping

while blood ran from both nostrils into his mouth. I wanted to punch him again – to go on punching for all the times he'd bullied me, and for Dad, and Cocky, but I couldn't. We stood looking at each other, and then he snorted and shook his head and flung himself at me and I found myself flat on my back with the bully kneeling on my chest. Blood from his nose was dripping onto my face, so I turned my head to one side.

I knew what he was going to do. His favourite trick when he had somebody down was to grab a double handful of his victim's hair, just above the ears, and bang his head to the ground again and again. Kenneth Smith in Standard Two had to have stitches after Simcox did that to him. I bucked and writhed but it was no use – I couldn't shake him off, so I screwed up my eyes and prepared for the worst.

I suppose if I gave you three guesses, you wouldn't guess what happened next. There I was with my eyes closed, waiting for the torture to start, and suddenly Clive Simcox burst into tears. As I opened my eyes to look at him, he sort of slid off me on to the ground and lay with his hands over his face, rocking himself and sobbing.

I didn't know what to do. I sat up and looked at him and after a bit I said, 'What's up?'

'My dad,' he choked. 'He's dead.'

As I mentioned, Simcox senior worked at the button factory. How could he be dead?

'Dead?' I gasped. 'How?'

'Yesterday. The raid on the aerodrome.'

'But – your dad's in the factory. What

75

was he doing at the aerodrome?'

'He wasn't on the aerodrome,' he sobbed.
'A stick of bombs fell short. One hit a house
near the factory.'

'Oh, yes – my mum mentioned it, but…'

'The house collapsed, see? Most of the
people got out but a little girl was trapped.
It was Dad's lunch break. He crawled into
the wreckage to get the kid, and the whole
lot fell on him.'

I understood then all right, but I still didn't know what to do so I laid a hand on his shoulder and said, 'He was a hero, your dad.' I thought it might help, but it did the opposite. A fresh howl burst from him and he cried, 'I know, and I was ashamed of him because he wasn't in the Army like everybody else's dad. I haven't even talked to him for months, and now it's too late.'

Well. Most families had somebody to mourn in those days. People tried to help

– meant to be kind – but in the end you just had to get through it. And you did get through it, but it changed you.

It changed Clive Simcox all right. The bullying stopped. He'd been acting tough to make up for his dad not being in the Army, see? He thought kids were sneering behind his back and maybe they were, some of them. People can be very cruel – kids especially. Anyway they gave Simcox senior a medal, and quite right too. Clive had to go to Buckingham Palace and be presented. That bucked him up a bit, but it didn't cancel out the thing that haunted him. Fifty years have gone by since then and he still wishes he'd been nicer to his dad. He doesn't go on about it, but I know because we're best friends. You know – like Britain and Germany. Makes you wonder why we had to fight in the first place, doesn't it?

Glossary

Brownings (page 49)

The eight machine guns carried in the wings of Hurricanes and Spitfires.

evacuated (page 13)

In 1939, many thousands of children were sent out of London and other cities because the authorities expected heavy bombing. The children were lodged with families in rural areas. This was called evacuation.

Guadeloupe triangular (page 11)

A postage stamp much coveted among

young collectors. Fictitious.

Junkers 88 (page 71)

Junkers Ju 88, a German bomber.

rationed (page 32)

The war caused food shortages. Meat, tea, sugar, butter and many other foods were rationed. Each person was entitled to so much each week and no more. They had to use coupons to get their rations. The system was intended to ensure fair shares for all.

requisitioned (page 16)

In times of emergency, governments can seize things they need without paying for them. Usually, owners are promised the return of their property, or payment, when the emergency is over. In the 1930s and '40s the British government acquired a great deal of farmland on which to build airfields and military camps. They requisitioned it.

shellshock (page 18)
Severe nervous damage caused by horrific experiences in the trenches of World War I.

togs (page 26)
Clothes.

tommy guns (page 18)
Early submachine guns, once favoured by American gangsters.

wizard (page 47)
A 1940s expression meaning good, exciting, wonderful (like great, awesome, cool, mega, wicked, etc.).

Wooden Cross (page 28)

The cross on a grave. Jim is making a wry joke.

yarning (page 42)

Telling tales of their adventures.

From the Author

Jim's friend is a fighter pilot, a national hero. Jim is proud to know Cocky, but there's another sort of hero in his life: the sort who performs no dashing deeds but carries on hoovering and washing up as if nothing bad has happened to her. Her picture's never in the paper, and she gets no medals. Heroes like Cocky are only seen in wartime, but heroes like Jim's mum are all around us, all the time. You probably know one. Tell us about her, or him, and what makes them a hero to you.

As Jim grows older, he finds that enemies sometimes turn into friends. Clive Wilcox is one, Germany is another. Why do you think people become enemies in the first place? Could we stop it happening? How would you try to do this?

Robert Swindells

Robert Swindells left school at the age of fifteen and joined the Royal Air Force at seventeen-and-a-half. After his discharge from the RAF he worked at a variety of jobs, then trained and worked as a teacher before becoming a full-time writer. Robert lives with his wife, Brenda, on the Yorkshire moors. He has written many books for young people, and won a number of awards; including the prestigious Carnegie Medal and the Sheffield Book Award for *Stone Cold*, the Children's Book Award and the Other Award for his novel *Brother in the*

Land, and three more Red House Awards with *Room 13*, *Nightmare Stairs* and, most recently, *Blitzed*.

Collect the World War II Trilogy!

ISBN 978-1-78270-162-0

It's summer 1944, and doodlebugs – Hitler's deadly flying bombs – are raining down on the city, bringing fear and destruction. Nobody is safe and the next attack may come at any moment...

When it seems like the war will tear Sandy's family apart, can they find the courage to survive?

Read all the books in the series!

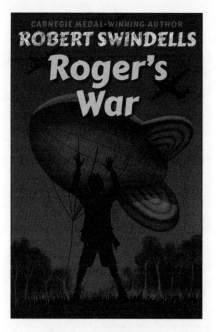

ISBN 978-1-78270-163-7

When pilots of the USAAF are based near Roger's village, they soon become his heroes. All his life Roger has dreamed of being special, just like them, but even his mum thinks he's a little bit daft.

Then one night Roger is put to the ultimate test. Can he avert danger? Could his actions change his life forever?

ALSO BY ROBERT SWINDELLS...
THE OUTFIT

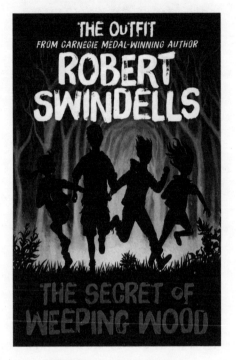

ISBN 978-1-78270-053-1

The Outfit had never really believed
the stories about the ghosts of Weeping
Wood – until now. But as they investigate
the mysterious cries, truth suddenly
becomes stranger – and more
terrifying – than fiction!

READ THE EXCITING ADVENTURES OF
THE OUTFIT

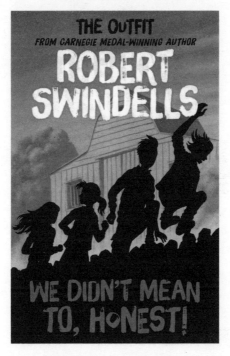

ISBN 978-1-78270-054-8

Miserable Reuben Kilchaffinch is going
to fill in Froglet Pond, and he won't let
anything, or anyone, get in his way.
The Outfit are desperate to save the pond
and its wildlife and they plan to stop
Kilchaffinch – at any cost!

LOOK OUT FOR ALL THE ADVENTURES OF
THE OUTFIT

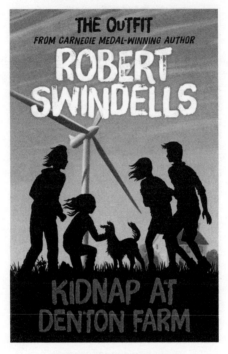

ISBN 978-1-78270-055-5

When Farmer Denton has a wind turbine
built on his farm, little does he know what
trouble it will bring. After one of them goes
missing, The Outfit must solve the mystery of
the malicious caller – and fast – if they ever
want to see their friend again!

UNCOVER THRILLING MYSTERIES WITH
THE OUTFIT

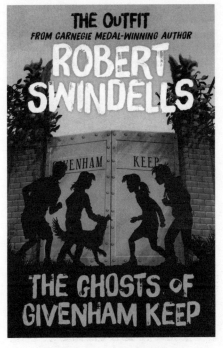

ISBN 978-1-78270-056-2

Steel gates and barbed wire have
been put up around the old mansion in
Weeping Wood. Someone has something to
hide and The Outfit intend to find out what.
But their innocent investigation soon
takes a sinister turn...

COLLECT ALL SIX BOOKS IN THE SERIES!
THE OUTFIT

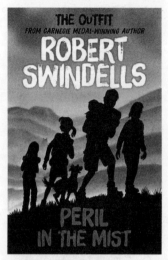

ISBN 978-1-78270-057-9

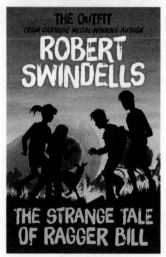

ISBN 978-1-78270-058-6